Good Luck, Ronald Morgan!

Good Luck, Ronald Morgan!

by Patricia Reilly Giff

illustrated by Susanna Natti

Viking

I wish to acknowledge my gratitude to the
MacDowell Colony, a haven of warmth, support,
and serenity for writers.   P. R. G.

VIKING
Published by the Penguin Group
Penguin Books USA Inc., 375 Hudson Street, New York, New York 10014, U.S.A.
Penguin Books Ltd, 27 Wrights Lane, London W8 5TZ, England
Penguin Books Australia Ltd, Ringwood, Victoria, Australia
Penguin Books Canada Ltd, 10 Alcorn Avenue, Toronto, Ontario, Canada M4V 3B2
Penguin Books (N.Z.) Ltd, 182–190 Wairau Road, Auckland 10, New Zealand
Penguin Books Ltd, Registered Offices: Harmondsworth, Middlesex, England

First published in 1996 by Viking, a division of Penguin Books USA Inc.

1   3   5   7   9   10   8   6   4   2

Text copyright © Patricia Reilly Giff, 1996   Illustrations copyright © Susanna Natti, 1996
All rights reserved

LIBRARY OF CONGRESS CATALOGING-IN-PUBLICATION DATA
Giff, Patricia Reilly.
Good luck, Ronald Morgan / by Patricia Reilly Giff ; illustrated by Susanna Natti.   p.   cm.
Summary : Ronald Morgan needs lots of luck not only to train the dog which he just
received for his birthday but also to win the friendship of his new neighbor.
ISBN 0-670-86303-3 (hardcover)
[1. Dogs—Fiction. 2. Friendship—Fiction.]   I. Natti, Susanna, ill. II. Title.
PZ7.G3626Go 1996 [E]—dc20   96-15133 CIP AC

Manufactured in China   Set in New Aster

For Dennis Lawlor, my favorite school principal,
who loves children . . . and dogs!
—P. R. G.

To Winston
and his family,
Ronnie, Arnie, Rebecca, and Ben
—S. N.

It was hot. It was sticky.

It was summer.

My friend Michael was away
at the lake.

But I had a book from my teacher, Miss Tyler,
and a new good-luck birthday dog.

"Shake hands, Lucky," I said.

But Lucky wouldn't shake hands.
He was barking at a truck.
The truck stopped next door.
Someone was moving in.
I hoped it was a boy.
Lucky hoped it was a dog.

It was a girl with a cat.

They poked their heads over the fence.

"My name is Kelly," she said.

Lucky raced back and forth.

"Want to be friends?" I asked.

The cat hissed.

Kelly didn't answer.

She was chasing her cat

up the street.

"Come back, Tiger!" she was yelling.

I began to read the book.
Some dogs can do tricks or swim.
Some dogs can even herd sheep, I read.
Every animal is good at something,
and that's the important thing.
"Great," I said.
Lucky thought the book was great, too.
He started to chew on the cover.

The next morning, I said to Lucky,
"Maybe you can play ball."
I could see Kelly across the fence.
"Want to play?" I asked.
But she was trying to get her cat down.

I threw the ball to Lucky.
"Catch it!" I called.
Lucky jumped the fence.
He came back with the cat
instead of the ball.

Miss Tyler was sitting in the park.
Lucky stopped to pick up a baseball cap
that was lying on the ground,
and then we ran to meet her.
"Maybe Lucky will shake hands," I said.
But he wanted to sit on Miss Tyler's lap.
His paws were a little muddy, though,
and he left prints on her new sweatsuit.
Miss Tyler gave him a pat.
"Have you read the *Train Your Pet* book yet?"
she asked me.

On the way home, I waved to Kelly.
Kelly didn't wave back.
She was crawling under her bushes
looking for something.
Tiger was up on top.
Maybe she was looking
for something, too.
Lucky didn't stop to watch.
He was tossing the cap in the air
and catching it.

I looked at the book again,
while Lucky ate the grass.
Be kind to your pet, it said.
Find out what he's good at.
Make sure you praise him.

I gave him the cap to play with.
"Good dog," I said,
and turned the page.

Just then something hit me in the eye.
Dirt was flying through the air.
It was Lucky digging under the fence.
A minute later, he was in Kelly's yard.
But the cat wasn't.

She had jumped through
the open garage window.
I crawled under the fence
to get Lucky,
but I fell over Kelly.

"Want to be friends?" I asked again.
But Kelly was marching into the
garage, and I had to take Lucky home.

I sat in the kitchen.

Lucky chewed the table leg.

I asked my mother,

"How can I be friends with Kelly?"

My mother thought for a minute.

"Maybe you could invite her for lunch."

And I said, "That's just what I was thinking."

I took a breath.

"I don't think she's friends with Lucky, either."

My mother frowned at Lucky.

"Maybe you should train him."

I ran to get the book.
Make sure your pet knows
what you want him to do, it said.
"Roll over, Lucky," I told him.
I rolled over to show him how.
First Lucky buried his cap.
Then he rolled into my mother's flowers.

But Kelly hadn't seen.
She was looking up.
"Want to come to lunch tomorrow? It's
peanut butter and cookies," I said.
Kelly didn't answer me.
"Tiger!" she yelled. "Get
down from there!"
"Bring Tiger, too," I called.

The next morning, Lucky was digging
under a bush.
"Maybe they're coming," I told him.
Lucky looked up.
Then he went back to digging,
this time under a rock.
I went inside for sandwiches and cookies.
I brought out a shovel to fill in Lucky's holes.

Kelly came over the fence.
"Shake hands, Lucky," I said.
But Lucky was digging again.
My mother brought out the napkins.
She brought out pet food, too.
Kelly said, "I'm trying to train my cat."

I looked up at Tiger.

"She must be good at something," I said.

"And that's the important thing."

I looked back at Lucky.

"Don't dig in the grass," I whispered.

Lucky started another hole.
He pulled out the cap,
and put it at Kelly's feet.
"I can't believe it," she said.
"You taught Lucky to find my cap . . .
my special baseball cap!"

I opened my mouth. "I didn't—"
"Want to be friends?" she asked.
I took a bite of my sandwich,
and nodded. "Sure."
"Maybe you can help train Tiger, too," she said.
I crossed my fingers. "Maybe," I said.

Just then I saw someone coming.
"Good news," I said. "Michael's back."
Michael had a huge dog with him.
"Shake hands, Spot," he said.

Tiger streaked up the oak tree.
Lucky streaked through the
hole in the fence.
And Spot came last.
"I just found out," I said.
"Tiger is good at climbing."
But Kelly didn't have time to answer.
Neither did Michael.

I grabbed the book.

"Now let's find out what Spot can do."